To Ashley,

Love,
Carmen

TACKY
the Penguin

Helen Lester
Illustrated by Lynn Munsinger

Houghton Mifflin Company

Boston 1988

Books by Helen Lester and illustrated by Lynn Munsinger

Books by Helen Lester and illustrated by Lynn Munsinger

The Wizard, the Fairy, and the Magic Chicken

It Wasn't My Fault

A Porcupine Named Fluffy

Pookins Gets Her Way

Tacky the Penguin

Library of Congress Cataloging-in-Publication Data

Lester, Helen.

Tacky the penguin/Helen Lester; illustrated by Lynn Munsinger.
p. cm.
Summary: Tacky the penguin does not fit in with his sleek and graceful companions, but his odd behavior comes in handy when hunters come with maps and traps.
ISBN 0-395-45536-7
[1. Penguins—Fiction. 2. Behavior—Fiction. 3. Individuality—Fiction.] I. Munsinger, Lynn, ill. II. Title.
PZ7.L56285Tac 1988 87-30684
[E]—dc19 CIP
AC

Printed in Italy

NI 10 9 8 7 6 5 4 3 2 1

There once lived a penguin.
His home was a nice icy land he shared
with his companions.

His companions were named
Goodly, Lovely, Angel, Neatly, and Perfect.

His name was Tacky.
Tacky was an odd bird.

Every day Goodly, Lovely, Angel, Neatly, and Perfect
greeted each other quietly and politely.

Tacky greeted them with a hearty slap on the back
and a loud "What's happening?"

Goodly, Lovely, Angel, Neatly, and Perfect always marched

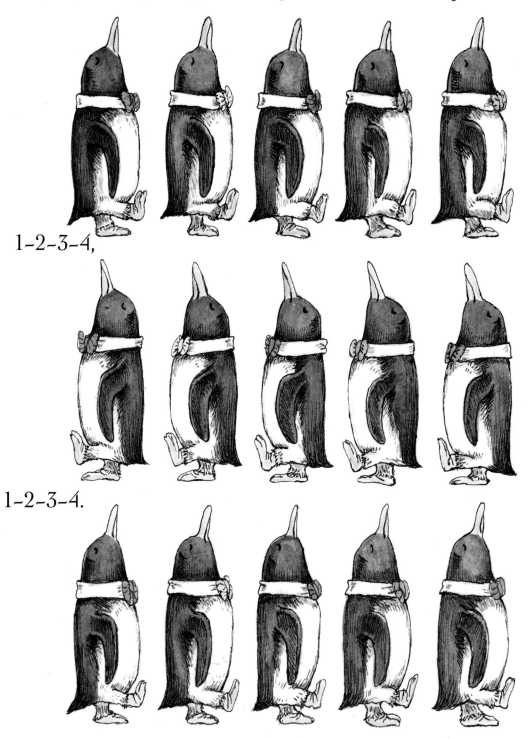

1–2–3–4,

1–2–3–4.

Tacky always marched 1–2–3,

4–2,

3–6–0,

2½,

0.

His companions were graceful divers.

Tacky liked to do splashy cannonballs.

Goodly, Lovely, Angel, Neatly, and Perfect
always sang pretty songs like
"Sunrise on the Iceberg."

Tacky always sang songs like
"How Many Toes Does a Fish Have?"
Tacky was an odd bird.

One day the penguins heard the *thump . . . thump . . . thump*
of feet in the distance.
This could mean only one thing.
Hunters had come.

They came with maps and traps and rocks and locks, and they were rough and tough. As the *thump . . . thump . . . thump* drew closer, the penguins could hear the growly voices chanting,

"We're gonna catch some pretty penguins,
And we'll march 'em with a switch,
And we'll sell 'em for a dollar,
And get rich, rich, RICH!"

Goodly, Lovely, Angel, Neatly, and Perfect
ran away in fright.

They hid behind a block of ice.

Tacky stood alone.

The hunters marched right up to him, chanting,

"We're gonna catch some pretty penguins,
And we'll march 'em with a switch,
And we'll sell 'em for a dollar,
And get rich, rich, RICH!"

"What's happening?" blared Tacky, giving one hunter an especially hearty slap on the back.

They growled, "We're hunting for penguins.
That's what's happening."

"PENNNNGUINS?" said Tacky. "Do you mean those birds that march neatly in a row?"
And he marched,

1-2-3,

4-2,

3-6-0,

2½,

0.

The hunters looked puzzled.

"Do you mean those birds that dive so gracefully?"
Tacky asked.

And he did a splashy cannonball.
The hunters looked wet.

"Do you mean those birds that sing such pretty songs?"
Tacky began to sing, and from behind the block of ice
came the voices of his companions,
all singing as loudly and dreadfully as they could.

"HOW MANY TOES DOES A FISH HAVE?

AND HOW MANY WINGS ON A COW?

I WONDER. YUP,

I WONDER."

The hunters could not stand the horrible singing.
This could not be the land of the pretty penguins.
They ran away with their hands clasped tightly over their ears,
leaving behind their maps and traps and rocks and locks,
and not looking at all rough and tough.

Goodly, Lovely, Angel, Neatly, and Perfect hugged Tacky.
Tacky was an odd bird but a very nice bird to have around.